The

Christmas

FELICIA BOND

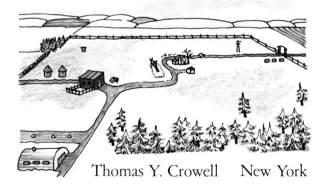

Thomas Y. Crowell   New York

The Chicks' Christmas
Copyright © 1983 by Felicia Bond
Printed in Singapore. All rights reserved.

Library of Congress Cataloging in Publication Data
Bond, Felicia.
    The chicks' Christmas.

    Summary: Two baby chicks want very badly to have a
Christmas tree, but the grumpy hens refuse to leave the
coop to get one.

    [1. Christmas—Fiction.   2. Christmas trees—Fiction.
3. Chickens—Fiction]   I. Title.
PZ7.B63666Ch   1983   [E]   82-45918
ISBN 0-694-00156-2
ISBN 0-690-04333-3 (lib. bdg.)

It was the week before Christmas,

and Chick and Pea wanted a Christmas
tree *very* badly.

Inside the coop, twelve grumpy hens
said no,

because they didn't want to leave the
coop to get one.

"A tree can't lay our eggs," said the wisest hen.

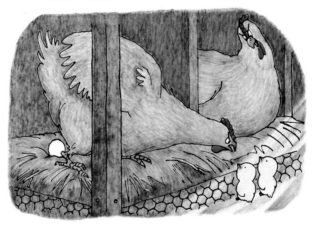

"We've never had a tree before," said the most stubborn hen.

"You know we never leave the coop,"
said the stuffiest hen.

But Chick and Pea wanted a tree, one
that almost touched the ceiling,

with bits of light that danced across its branches,

and a star on top that glowed

like a thousand.

So they sneaked out of the coop

and found one.

They were sure the hens would like it.

But the hens said, "Take that pathetic little branch back to where you found it!"

Chick and Pea were sure the hens had
not seen their tree clearly.

"It's *very* dark in the coop," Chick said.

"If only we could get them outside!"
said Pea.

"We could tell them we saw an angel!"
said Chick. "THAT would get them out!"

"Let's do it," said Pea.

The hens rushed out of the coop.

They oohed and ahhed and stared.

They wanted a Christmas tree

very badly.

"One with a star on top!" said the
wisest hen.

From that time on,

the hens left the coop to look at
the trees,

at every time of year,

and especially at Christmas.